In and Out the Window

CHILDHOOD IN VERSE

by Jacqueline Bandel

Illustrations by Camille LaPointe

Ambrly Books
1995

On Melly Rosen's computer, my husband, Bob Somers, typed and retyped his computer-illiterate wife's manuscript, offering support and suggestions throughout this endeavor. And with alacrity and skill, Tia Rosen proofread the manuscript. Sara Glaser then arranged the text and illustrations with her magic fingers. Adding to this circle of support was Joan Cohn, who was my constant grammarian, and artist and friend, Katherine Tillotson, whose assistance with color was invaluable. My generous thank you to Melly and Tia, to Sara, Joan, Katherine, and especially Bob, and to illustrator Camille LaPointe for her unflagging patience, cheerfulness and encouragement from the inception of our work together, to completion of this book.

The illustrations of young people in this book are drawn from photographs of my children and grandchildren.

Copyright © 1995 Jaqueline Bandel

All rights reserved. No part of this book may be reproduced in any form or by any means without the written permission of the author.

First edition.
Printed in the United States of America.

Amberly Books
c/o Regent Press
6020-A Adeline Street
Oakland, CA 94608

Library of Congress Cataloging-in-Publication Data

Bandel, Jacqueline
    In and out the window : childhood in verse / by Jacqueline Bandel
    illustrations by Camille LaPointe. -- 1st ed.
    ISBN 0-916147-46-0 -- ISBN 0-916147-45-2 (pbk.)
    1. Children's poetry, American.   [1. American poetry.]
 I. LaPointe, Camille, ill.   II. Title.
PS3552.A4752   1995   95-25106
811'.54--dc20   CIP
                                                                                      AC

*This book is for
Two quartets, plus one,
And additional grandchildren
Yet to come.*

*The first quartet,
Todd, Sandy, Scott, Jay,
Are my children, now grown,
Who are wending their way*

*As parents of Alison,
Rachel, Michelle,
Jamie and Kyle—
And the numbers may swell.*

*For you, my dear family,
I have written these poems.
May they bring you much pleasure.
May they brighten your homes.*

Contents

At The Beach 1
Guess Again 2
Fair Trade 3
Chicken Soup 4
My Best Friends 6
Three, Two, One—Blast Off! 7
The Pine Tree 8
At The Zoo 9
Dancing 10
Teatime 11
Abbit the Rabbit 12
Rachel's Good-Bad Week 14
Autumn Leaves 16
I'm A Boy! 17
A Snail Tale 18
Pretending 20
On Being Three 21
Tickety Boo 22

The Worm 23
Sleep Talking 24
It's Spring 25
Wondering................................26
Under the Big Top 27
Anticipation..............................28
A Foggy Day in San Francisco 30
Who Wins?................................32
Toys 33
Moon Beams 34
Finders Keepers 36
Sugar and Spice 37
Cake Baking 38
Round Trip 39
The New Puppy 40
Places 42
Dreams 43

At The Beach

When I run barefoot in the sand
Or build a castle in the air,
I do it very quietly
So no one knows I'm there.

Guess Again

Today I'm going to find a rose
That's blooming red and full
And take some scissors to the stem,
Then cut and give a pull.

I'll tiptoe in to Mother.
I shall not make a sound.
I'll put my hands across her eyes
And say, "Guess what I found?"

And Mom will say, "A lizard?"
Or "A beetle?" or "A snake?"
And I will show her my red rose
And laugh at her mistake.

Fair Trade

Scotty has a tricycle.
He rides up hill and down.
A tricycle, a tricycle,
He rides it into town.

He rides it to go shopping.
He rides it through the park.
He rides it in the neighborhood,
But never after dark.

His tricycle is shiny.
His tricycle is new.
But when he's one year older,
Here's what he says he'll do.

He says he'll take his tricycle,
His well-used three-wheeled trike,
And pedal to the toy store
To trade it for a bike.

Chicken Soup

I'm eating chicken soup with noodles.
Mother says I'll love it oodles.
But you know what I think is nice?
Eating chicken soup with rice.

I'm eating meatballs with spaghetti.
For twenty minutes it's been ready.
It's difficult to say just why,
But I prefer zucchini pie.

Now I'm eating macaroni.
It tastes like yesterday's bologna.
There's no doubt I'd rather eat
French fries for my dinner treat.

Stew with carrots—that's what's served.
It's not what I think I deserved.
I always thought my mother knew
I must have mushrooms in my stew.

Cold sliced veggies in my lunch box.
Healthful food that tastes like wet socks.
What I want—let me confide—
Is cakes and cookies stacked inside.

Cupcakes filled with goopy glop.
Vanilla frosting on the top.
Vanilla frosting—big mistake!
I want chocolate on my cake.

So, I'm back to soup with noodles.
It's quite respected among foodles.
But here is my esteemed advice.
Try your chicken soup with rice.

My Best Friends

A-to-zees are all around.
They're in the sky and on the ground.
With reddish eyes and greenish hair,
You don't see one; you see a pair.

A-to-zees don't like to walk.
They can squeak, but cannot talk.
They like to dance and run and play.
They stay awake both night and day.

A-to-zees are all around.
To see them you can't make a sound.
For if a person's voice they hear,
Just like THAT, they disappear.

They never have to go to schools.
They are happy to be fools.
They eat a funny kind of food
They grow when they are in the mood.

Now A-to-zees are only real,
Depending on the way you feel.
I made them up just to be silly
One winter day when it was chilly.

And although they are "just pretend,"
A-to-zees are my best friends.

Three, Two, One—Blast Off!

Mother said that I could ride
A rocket to the moon.
And if I am especially good,
I hope that I go soon.

I have my space suit ready,
And when I climb inside,
I'll signal to the pilot,
Then sit back for the ride.

We'll rise above the ocean.
We'll head straight for the stars.
But if the pilot goes off course,
We might crash into Mars!

The Pine Tree

I'm a pine tree
Tall and proud.
And when it's windy
I talk out loud.

At The Zoo

Kangaroos
And bears in lairs
And lions
Prancing 'round in pairs
And elephants
And gawky gnus
Are animals
We see in zoos.

Dancing

I'm hoping you can tell me
How my Daddy always knows
That when it's time for dinner
I'm here dancing on my toes.

I'm pointing and I curtsy
In my tutu made of lace.
Still, Dad wants me at the table
With the family, saying grace.

I'm leaping and I'm bowing
The way dancers do.
I'm stretching to the ceiling,
And my tutu's stretching, too.

My ballet slippers lead me
Down the hall and up a stair.
I'm jumping and I'm balancing.
My arms swirl in the air.

I'm twirling and I'm turning.
I'm spinning around and 'round.
I'm reeling, really reeling.
Oops—I'm on the ground!

Teatime

We're having our tea,
Jamie and I.
We're here in the garden.
The cat's standing by.

We're having some tea,
Jamie and me.
I'm pouring the milk
'Neath the apricot tree.

We invited our cousins:
Jay, Kyle, Michelle.
Rachel and Alison
Are coming as well.

Perhaps we'll include
Todd, Sandy, and Scott.
There's plenty of tea
In our silver teapot.

We're like the grownups,
My cousins and me,
With white linen napkins
And peppermint tea.

We're like the big folks,
My cousins and I,
Having mint tea and crumpets,
Oh, and Eskimo Pie.

Abbit the Rabbit

Abbit the rabbit
Had the bad habit
Of stealing ripe carrots
And such.

He knew that he shouldn't.
He promised he wouldn't.
But his promises
Didn't mean much.

From gardens in front,
From gardens behind,
From neighbors
On his street and next,

He stole in the morning.
He stole in the night,
Leaving everyone,
Young and old, vexed.

Abbit the rabbit
Deplored his bad habit.
(It embarrassed his mom
And his dad.)

He knew it was wrong.
But as he hopped along,
This is the reason
He had:

I follow my nose,
And wherever it goes,
I find
That I go along, too.

Biological need?
Anatomical greed?
Alas,
Nothing else can I do.

Indeed, I do try
To pass carrots by,
But their taste
Is unduly sublime.

So I take at least four.
And when I want more,
I return
To the scene of the crime.

Oh, I want to be good.
And a wise rabbit would
Think only
Of good things to do.

And unless in disguise,
He should heed neighbors' cries,
Lest he become
Rabbit stew.

Rachel's Good-Bad Week

Monday is here.
I'll call Joyce McLear.
She'll pick up my Rachel,
Who lives very near

And walk her to school
If the weather is clear,
Unless it should rain
And the sky disappear.

Tuesday has come.
Rachel is glum.
She must go to the doctor
For an ache in her ear.

It's infected and oh,
Bad bacteria grow
Inside where it's warm
And the follicles glow.

Wednesday, it's time
To call Doctor MacLime.
He'll check Rachel's symptoms
And quiet her fear.

No one is happy.
Rachel is blue.
The family is worried.
They're afraid now it's flu.

On Thursday, as well,
Rachel's glands start to swell.
Her temperature rises.
Doctor Mac gets in gear.

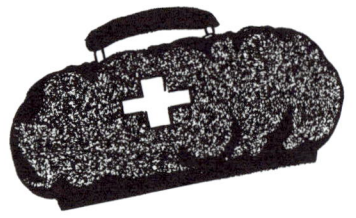

Dad buys a prescription.
Joyce McLear starts to pray.
And Rachel stays tucked
In her bed all the day.

Now, Friday's turn.
Those germs start to churn.
From the antibiotic
They curdle in fear.

Saturday flies.
Ah, Rachel's bright eyes!
What seems like the flu
Is decidedly through.

Doctor Mac stops to check.
(Yes, the germs are a wreck.)
And the patient proclaims
She's a true musketeer.

Can you imagine
The joy, the delight,
When Rachel's high fever
Is normal that night?

Sunday is fun.
Some resting, some sun.
Three pills left to take
So no germs reappear.

The promise of school,
One day at a time,
Brings to a close
This good- bad-week rhyme.

Autumn Leaves

The fall leaves crinkle
As you sweep
Them all together
In a heap.

They crunch and make
A cracking sound
As you stamp them
On the ground.

Crinkling
Cracking
Crunching
Leaves.
Autumn voices
Sure to please.

I'm A Boy!

I'm a boy.
I take the heat.
I never walk.
I stamp my feet.

I'm a boy.
I'm very strong.
I outrun girls
All day long.

I ride the range
On my white horse.
I lasso steers
Quite fast, of course.

I throw a ball
Beyond the park.
I'm not afraid
To ride a shark.

I shoot at stars
With bow and quiver.
I toss *small* fish
Back to the river.

For I'm a boy.
And I am rough!
And I am big.
And I am tough.

I work all day
Without a care—
Then sleep all night
With Teddy bear.

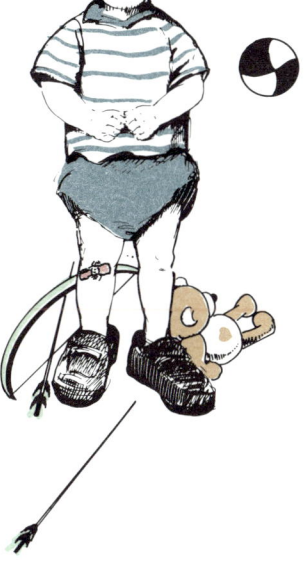

A Snail Tale

Have you ever seen
(And please do not lie)
A snail with a tail of a quail
Go by?

Well, I have.
I saw one
Last week
In the sand.

I touched it
And lifted it
Into
My hand.

It slithered
And quivered
And oh,
What a sight.

It churned,
And it turned,
And I squealed
With delight.

Then slowly I set it
Inside my sand pail
And took it to Mother
To tell her the tale.

Proudly, I handed
My mother the pail.
She looked inside....
Hey! Where is that snail?

All that remained
Inside my sand pail
Were a few grains of sand
Shaken off the snail's tail.

Now I know
That I saw it,
But to you
It must seem

That my snail
With the tail
Of a quail
Is a dream.

Pretending

Look! I am an airplane.
I'm buzzing through the sky.
I'm skimming over mountains
And watching clouds go by.

Watch, I am a steamship.
I'm churning waters blue.
I have a rugged captain
Who gives orders to the crew.

Wait! I am a tractor.
I'm moving dirt around.
I scoop it up and dump it
And reorganize the ground.

Listen…I'm an orchestra.
My music can astound.
Six drums, four harps, a clarinet—
You can't *believe* the sound.

Now I am a panda.
I'm painted black and white.
But sometimes I'm a scary witch
Who skims the moon at night.

Oh, I am so many things—
A bird, a buzzing bee.
But when I'm through pretending,
I'm glad that I am me.

On Being Three

I'm three now.
Just look at ME now.
First of all
I am so tall
That I can throw
A rubber ball
FIFTY feet—
Up to the sky!

Can you catch anything that high?

Tickety Boo

I have a toy that's very new.
This special toy goes
Tickety...BOO!

I wind it tight,
And when I do,
The faster it goes
Tickety...BOO!

If I should wind it extra fast,
Right up to the very last,
I guess then I would
Break the spring
And end up with
An OLD plaything.

The Worm

In my hand I have a worm.
I hold it tight and make it squirm.
But it is very tiny, so
I think that I shall let it go.

Sleep Talking

At night, when Mom has gone to sleep,
I rise from bed without a peep
And sit upon my window sill,
When all the world is very still.

I see a star that twinkles bright
And ask it if it shines its light
On any other wakeful child
Whose curiosity is riled.

I ask Big Dipper if it knows
Why it rains and how it snows
And why the white clouds floating by
Are sometimes low and sometimes high.

Now Big Dipper calls to me.
(I wonder if the ships at sea
and all the fishes in the ocean
are aware of the commotion?)

For I don't want my Mom to hear.
(Her bedroom door is very near.)
She would send me back to bed,
Tuck me in, up to my head,
And say so loud the stars would hear,
"Back to sleep and quickly, dear!"

It's Spring

Hyacinths, crocus and gold daffodils
Are coloring gardens and painting the hills.

Fuzz from the seeds of the cottonwood trees
Willow in air, swaying high in the breeze.

Dripping-wet calves and lean-legged foals
Are tamping the meadows and grazing the knolls.

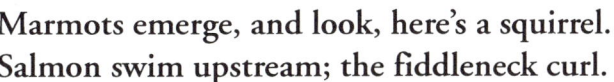

Marmots emerge, and look, here's a squirrel.
Salmon swim upstream; the fiddleneck curl.

Soft worms are squirming; a robin takes wing.
An iced pond is cracking. The trees add a ring.

Dogwoods are budding; the mockingbirds sing.
A thawed earth is bursting and welcoming spring.

Wondering

When springtime comes and flowers bloom,
I go outside so I have room
To watch the white clouds floating by
And wonder why they're up so high.

I wonder if they ever fall
Into trees whose limbs are tall.
And if a mountain blocked their way
Would they come back another day?

Under the Big Top

Did you see the circus
Pass through town last night?
I sneaked under the Big Top
To watch by pale moonlight.

I saw a jolly fat man.
He weighed three hundred pounds.
I watched the circus elephants
Jump hoops and over mounds.

The tightrope walkers scared me.
I hoped they wouldn't fall.
I loved the lion tamer
And the seal playing ball.

I looked at horses prancing.
I kissed a funny clown.
I watched the trapeze lady
Swing up and then swing down.

Then the clown gave me some popcorn.
It was special circus popcorn.
And I think I liked the popcorn
The very best of all.

Anticipation

When I am big—at least thirteen,
I'll never keep my bedroom clean.

The cat will sleep inside my bed,
All covered up, except her head.

I'll leave my clothing on the floor
And sometimes slam my bedroom door.

At thirteen years, not one day more,
I'll never do another chore.

And by then I will know, for sure,
There's not a problem I can't cure.

When I'm thirteen, so smart and wise,
At noontime, I shall plan to rise.

I'll watch TV both night and day,
And stash my homework far away.

When I am grown and in my teens,
I'll go to church in faded jeans.

I won't wear socks or proper shoes.
In fact, I'll do just what I choose.

But I'm just nine, so I must do
EVERYTHING Mom tells me to.

A Foggy Day in San Francisco

In a city whose Golden Gate
Greets each new day,
Where curlicue streets
Rendezvous with the bay,

With our out-of-town guests
(My dad was their host),
We drove to the beach,
Where the shore meets the coast.

There we sat on a bench
By a trail to the ocean
To watch tall waves break
In their rhythmic motion

And listen to fog horns
Warn sailors: BEWARE,
The sounds sifting through
The thickened, moist air.

Shhhh, those are seals
Whose barking we hear.
Slap, splash—they and their
Slippery pups disappear.

Look up, there's a pelican
High overhead,
With a fish in its beak
That might drop on my head!

Just beyond, circle gulls,
Whose habits, I fear,
Are to steal food from tourists
Who eat on the pier.

We walk with our guests
On sand paths to the shore.
But our voices get drowned
By the ocean's great roar.

It is time to go home.
The sun has now set.
Its oranges and yellows
And reds are all wet

From ribbons of fog.
The sky is ablaze.
Ah, one of those
Near unforgettable days

In a city where golden hills
Fade into grey,
In a city whose scenery
Shows off, every day.

Who Wins?

When I eat dinner
It's always a race
To see which gets more
My tummy or face.

Toys

Little kids
Have store-made toys.
But often
They would rather play
(On a dull or sunny day)
With pots and pans
And old tin cans,
And logs and dogs
And slippery frogs,
Or ropes and nails
And slimy snails,
Or even with
Old garbage pails.

Moon Beams

We went for a ride
One bright night in June.
And I noticed we seemed
To be chasing the moon.

But on the way home,
I clearly could see
That the Man in the Moon
Was following *me*.

Now isn't it strange?
Can it really be so—
That the Man in the Moon
Goes wherever I go?

I suppose he gets tired.
But when nighttime is done,
The kindly-faced moon
Is replaced by the sun.

Mister Moon sleeps all day,
While the sun shines its light.
Then the day-weary *sun*
Goes to bed for the night.

And year after year,
Day after day,
The moon lights our dreams
While the sun lights our play.

Finders Keepers

While walking in the warm sunlight,
I saw an object, flashy bright.
I picked it up.
To my surprise,
It had no arms.
It had no eyes.

It had no legs.
It had no nose.
It had no teeth,
No hands,
No clothes.

Instead it had
A dazzling glow.
But what it was
I did not know.

So I ran
And ran some more,
Until I saw our grocery store.

I showed the clerk
My new surprise
And watched the glow
Come to his eyes.

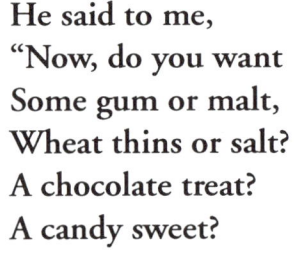

He said to me,
"Now, do you want
Some gum or malt,
Wheat thins or salt?
A chocolate treat?
A candy sweet?

Or maybe you would
Like a pencil,
Crayons, paper
And a stencil?"

Well, can you guess
Just what I found
That went around,
Around and 'round?

Fifty cents!
I was a King.
My fifty cents
Buys ANYTHING.

Sugar and Spice

Hop, hop
To the candy shop.
I think I'll stop
For a lollipop,
Or a jellybean
That's red and green,
Or a licorice stick
That I can lick,
And a peppermint
With just a hint
Of sugar and spice.

Aren't candy shops nice!

Cake Baking

The very best part
Of baking a cake
Is the generous lick
Of the batter I take.

Round Trip

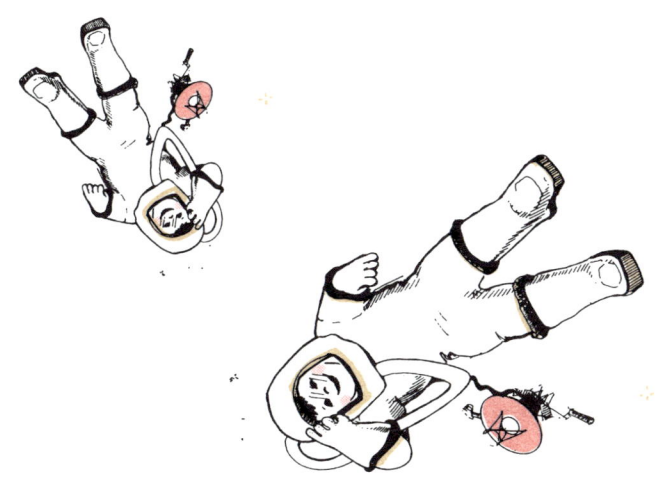

I took a ride.
I went so far.
I reached the sky.
I passed a star.

When I looked back
To give a nod,
I thought the world
Looked very odd.

The oceans were
Curved blurry spots;
The continents,
Rough polka dots.

The people were
Too small to see.
So I had stars
For company.

I landed
On the moon,
And then
I
  headed
    straight
      for
        home
          again.

The New Puppy

When Mom bathes
Scooter in the sink,
The water looks
Like mud and ink.

At Mom's left side
I like to stand,
With shampoo, towel
And brush in hand,

To watch the water
While it goes
By Scooter's eyes,
Right down his nose,

To see the water
Draining out,
To hear it blurping
Down the spout,

To watch my puppy
Shake and shake.
You should *see*
The mess he makes.

The water swings
And slings and flings.
It might as well
Have pilot's wings.

It floods the kitchen
High and low.
It leaves a lake
In which to row.

I take ten towels,
A sponge, a mop.
I wipe the floor
Until I drop.

Still, there's water
On the floor.
Oh look, here's more
And more, and MORE!

At last, I turn
To Mom to say,
"Enough of Scooter
For today."

Places

In between
The sky and street
Must be the place
Where fairies meet.

Dreams

My dreams come from the sandman.
He brings them by each night.
But he will only leave them
When my eyes are shut tight.

Once, when I was peeking
Out the window pane,
He wouldn't leave a single dream.
But he came back again.

Jacqueline Bandel is a native of San Francisco, California. She attended one semester of kindergarten at Winfield Scott grammar school before being whisked across the bay to Piedmont, where she completed her primary and secondary schooling. The University of California at Berkeley was next, followed by marriage, four children, editing, investigative reporting, feature and ghost writing. She lives in Berkeley with her husband in an empty-nested eight-bedroom house.